The Adventures of Alexander T. Frog

Michael Brian O'Hara

Archway Publishing books may be ordered through booksellers or by contacting:

Archway Publishing
1663 Liberty Drive
Bloomington, IN 47403
www.archwaypublishing.com
1 (888) 242-5904

Because of the dynamic nature of the Internet, any web addresses or links contained in this book may have changed since publication and may no longer be valid. The views expressed in this work are solely those of the author and do not necessarily reflect the views of the publisher, and the publisher hereby disclaims any responsibility for them.

Any people depicted in stock imagery provided by Thinkstock are models, and such images are being used for illustrative purposes only.
Certain stock imagery © Thinkstock.

ISBN: 978-1-4808-4458-2 (sc)
ISBN: 978-1-4808-4459-9 (e)

Print information available on the last page.

Archway Publishing rev. date: 3/14/2017

Now, Alexander T. Frog was no ordinary frog.

He was one of the smartest frogs there ever was.

The problem with being so smart was that
Alexander became bored too easily.

He could jump higher and farther than any other frog.

He could swim better and faster than any other frog.

He could catch flies better than any other frog.

But, being the best at doing frog things was
not enough for Alexander T. Frog.

He wanted to float like a butterfly.

He wanted to fly like a bird.

He wanted to swim under water like a fish.

He wanted to hop like a bunny rabbit.

He wanted to run fast like a horse.

So, one day the very smart Alexander T. Frog decided to talk with his animal friends to learn how he could do all the things they did.

The butterfly said, "Alexander, you are so smart you should know that you do so many more things than I can.

I cannot jump.

I cannot swim.

I cannot catch my food so easily.

You are much better off than me."

The bird said, "Alexander, you are so smart you should know you can do so many more things than I can.

I cannot jump.

I cannot swim, and

I must eat twice my weight in food.

All I can do is fly.

You are much better off than me."

The fish said, "Alexander, you are so smart you should know you can do so many more things than I can.

I cannot jump at all.

I cannot leave my pond.

All I can do is swim.

You are so much better off than me."

The rabbit said, "Alexander, you are so smart you should know you can do so many more things than I can.

I cannot swim.

I cannot jump as high and far as you do.

I cannot catch food as well as you can.

All I can do is hop.

You are so much better off than me."

The horse said, "Alexander, you are so smart you should know you can do so many more things than I can.

I cannot jump as high or as far as you do.

I cannot sit on a lilly pad in a pond.

All I can do is trot and gallop.

You are so much better off than me.

Finally, after talking with his animal friends, Alexander T. Frog decided that maybe he was really better off than his friends.

After all, the butterfly, the bird, the fish, the rabbit and the horse all convinced Alexander T. Frog that he could do so many more things than his friends.

THE END

CPSIA information can be obtained
at www.ICGtesting.com
Printed in the USA
LVOW05s2011120717
541167LV00024B/128/P